Who Is Tanksy?

Bev Katz Rosenbaum

ORCA BOOK PUBLISHERS

I find the hallway with my locker on the third try. "I like your nails," I make myself say to the girl with the locker next to mine. I really do like them. They're a calming ocean blue. I could use some calm.

She stares at me and says, "I wouldn't normally wear this color, but I'm raising awareness of pool deaths."

"Raising awareness...?"

"Of pool deaths." She looks down at my baggy pants and narrows her eyes. "Last year my cousin drowned at a party in a backyard swimming pool."

"Oh wow, I'm sorry. So you're raising money for..." I trail off, confused.

"I'm not raising *money*! I'm raising awareness!"

"Right," I say. "But how will painting your nails help—"

She cuts me off. "So you're *not* in favor of raising pool-death awareness?"

"Oh my god," I say quickly. "That's not what I meant. It's just—"

The second bell rings at that exact second. Blue Nail Girl and her gang of blue-nailed followers don't bother hearing me out.

And, of course, the only available seat in my homeroom, when I find it, is next to a blue-nailer.

I paste a smile on my face and say, "Anybody sitting here?"

The girl just looks at me and says, "I'm saving it."

Which means, of course, *You will never, ever sit beside me.*

As if the day isn't already off to an awesome start, my first class is gym. We play dodgeball. Just the game to make everybody feel warm and fuzzy. I'm hit in the head about three seconds in.

Our teacher, Ms. Fife, orders me to go sit in the bleachers. Which I happily do.

The rest of the day is full of more mean girls and barking teachers. Then drama class is canceled because there's an assembly.

I hang out at the back of the gym. I realize too late that I've plopped myself down beside Blue Nail Girl and a guy who looks like a smaller version of Principal Stone.

"You running for school president?" I hear Blue Nail Girl ask the guy as I get up to find a different spot.

"Ouch!"

Crap. I just stepped on Blue Nail Girl's toe.

"Sorry," I whisper.

"No worries, New Girl." She looks at me as if she's trying to decide whether I'm worthy of her attention.

I seem to pass the test. "I'm Samantha Pimm. And this is Aidan Stone."

Bingo. He's the principal's son.

"And you are…?"

"Tanya," I say. "Hi."

"Hi," Aidan says, sounding bored. "Tanya what?"

"Uh, Kofsky."

He knits his dark eyebrows together. "Kofsky sounds Jewish. Doesn't it, Marcus?"

Marcus, sitting on the other side of Aidan, is a big, blank-looking guy. "Yeah," he says.

"Yeah," says an even bigger awkward guy on the other side of Marcus. Wedged between them is the girl who wouldn't let me sit next to her earlier, Ashley. I get the feeling she and Marcus are "together."

"Shut up, Ox," says Aidan to the second guy, who, big as he is, deflates at Aidan's words.

Wow.

"You have dark skin," Aidan adds, turning back to me. "But you can't be Black. Black Jews aren't a thing."

Double wow. This guy is giving me chest pains. I can't believe people still say stuff like this after everything that has happened in the world.

I look at Samantha's ocean-blue nails and order myself to stay calm. "I'm not Black. I just have dark skin. But actually, there are lots of Black Jews. Ever heard of Drake?"

"Drake isn't Jewish."

"Uh, yeah, he is. He has a Jewish mother, and there's stuff in his songs—"

"No there isn't," he says, as if saying so makes it true. Why am I even wasting my breath on this guy? People like him don't listen.

"Oh my god, you can be such an idiot, Aidan," says Samantha.

Huh. So at least someone stands up to him. Though Samantha does it in that annoying *I love you anyhow* tone.

"But you'll still vote for me, right?" Aiden says, grinning and wiggling his eyebrows.

"If she's your only competition, yeah." Samantha points to a girl standing near the back door of the gym. A girl with straight black hair, glasses and great posture. She looks as pained as I am by the thought of spending one more second listening to Principal Stone. She's with a guy who is also frowning at Stone's long speech about Rules and Order.

"Who are they?" I ask Samantha.

"Dorothy Fairfield and Reza Golzar. Smart, change-the-world types. Reza doesn't say much. Writes a lot of award-winning essays on politics and stuff. Dorothy's going to run for school president, I think."

If she's a smart, change-the-world type, why wouldn't you vote for her? First I think it, then I say it.

Samantha shrugs. "I just can't see voting for someone I wouldn't be friends with, Tia."

"Tanya," I say. No response.

"You know, she isn't bad-looking," Aidan says, studying Dorothy. "If she dressed a little better, some guy might be interested." He turns to me. "You too, actually. What's with the baggy jeans?"

In addition to being an introvert, I am firmly nonviolent. But at this moment I suddenly imagine ripping Aidan Stone's eyebrows off.

Samantha points to her calf. "Leggings. Get some. Better yet, let me take you shopping, Talia. I'll give you a total makeover."

"Tanya." Again, no response. I'm so done with these two. "Sorry. Have to go. Bye."

I sneak out the back door of the gym and dash down the hall to escape. I spot Dorothy Fairfield and Reza Golzar by the main doors. I guess they couldn't take that assembly either. I grab the door as Reza lets go of it.

They turn to me, startled. Then their faces relax.

"You had as much fun in there as I did, huh?" I say.

Dorothy shoots me a sad smile. "I'm thinking of running for president. If you want to see some changes, vote for me."

"If that Stone Jr. is the only other choice, you can count on it."

"You're new here, right? I'm Dorothy. And this is Reza."

Reza just nods and smiles slightly.

"Tanya. Hey," I add, trying to sound casual, "feel like ice cream?" I point to the truck parked down the block.

"Sorry, have to get home," says Dorothy. "I have a lot of work to do." Reza nods again.

"Ah." I'm disappointed, but somehow it doesn't feel like a rejection. Especially when Dorothy adds, "See you around." Something in her eyes tells me it isn't that Dorothy doesn't want to be my friend. She's a girl who has a Calling, a girl who needs to Get Stuff Done.

"Yeah," I say. "See you."

I watch as Dorothy and Reza walk across the school parking lot and disappear around the first corner. I realize I'm smiling my first real smile of the day.

I look around to make sure no one's watching. Then I sneak around to the back of the school. And after another quick look, I take a can of spray paint and some stencils out of my backpack.

Chapter Two

Mom and Grandpa are looking out the window as I walk up to the door. As soon as I'm in, they usher me into the living room and start firing questions at me. God, is every day going to be like this?

We recently moved in with my Grandpa Gus, for a couple of reasons. He was having a bit of trouble managing on his own. But it's good for me and Mom too. Things haven't been easy for us since my dad died a few years ago. Giving up our apartment to live with Grandpa will ease some of the financial pressure on Mom.

I give them a quick summary of events, including Aidan's jerky comments about my background.

Mom gives me a hug. "I'm sorry, hon."

She's probably thinking what I'm thinking. We came from the area where my dad grew up, which has a lot of Jewish families. It wouldn't have occurred to either of us that moving to this neighborhood would be a big deal.

"But it's good that the principal's focus is on order," Grandpa says. "Nothing wrong with rules. Nothing at all. And it sounds like the boy was just curious about Jews." He gets up. "I have to go to the bathroom."

Mom watches him shuffle off. "He's been crusty all day." Her voice is a little high.

I'm not sure how to answer. Since we moved in, I've learned that my grandfather has a *lot* of opinions. And he isn't shy about sharing them. Mom sometimes tries to explain to him why the things he says are hurtful. But he usually just barks back that she's "too sensitive."

"I made your favorite for dinner," Mom says. "Black bean burgers and sweet potato fries."

"Awesome." If it were up to me, we'd eat vegetarian food at every meal.

At dinner, Grandpa starts talking about our new mayor, who sounds as mean and obsessed with "order" as Principal Stone.

"He says it like it is. That's why he got my vote."

"Really?" Mom asks. It's clear she's not as impressed.

"Yes, really, Nicole! What have you got against a guy who wants to help keep us safe?"

"Well, in fact, the crime rate in the area has been going down, Dad. I don't believe in scaring people to get votes."

Normally I'd help Mom out. But after my day, I'm feeling pretty bummed that she's brought us here to live. I don't really feel like defending her. I scramble up and mumble something about homework.

"On your first day?" Mom says, surprised.

"Yup." Well, nope, but she doesn't have to know that.

In my room I do a million sketches based on my impressions of the day. Then I start to feel bad for deserting Mom. I go back into the kitchen to help her clean up. While we load the dishwasher, I ask her if she got any writing done today.

"Actually, I did," she says. "Well, I jotted down a few ideas, at least."

"That's great, Mom."

My mom writes novels for teens. She's even published a few, but that was years ago. Now that our expenses are lower, she's determined to get back to creative writing.

"And what about your dating profile?" I ask. "Any messages?" Mom hasn't dated since Dad died. When we moved in with Grandpa, I told her she had no excuse now. That I could watch him when she went out. I'm already regretting the offer.

"Yeah, one. From a guy who doesn't work in publishing but who tried to tell me how publishing works."

I roll my eyes. Honestly. Guys who listen more than they talk, like Reza, seem few and far between.

When the kitchen is clean, I say goodnight to Mom. Then I do the same to Grandpa, who is in his favorite chair, watching a cop show.

Back in my room, I spend some time surfing Netflix on my laptop. Then I turn out the light. All the crap that happened on my first day comes flying back.

I force myself to focus on the one great part.

I can't wait to see what people think of my "contribution" to my new school.

Chapter Three

The beauty of being the kind of person whose name nobody can remember, and who nobody here knows, is that no one will ever suspect me. When I get to school the next day, a crowd has formed around the school's back wall. Everyone is admiring my painting of a Grinch-like figure herding a bunch of sheep into a large jail cell. Below it I stenciled *Keep*

Moving, People and my tag—*Tanksy*, a reference to famous street artist Banksy, of course. I love how he uses humor to talk about important stuff. And his images are super cool.

"Think it was somebody who goes here?" asks Ashley.

"Well, duh, obviously," Samantha says. "The question is, who?"

Next to her, Aidan is trying his best to look bored. But I detect a flicker of interest in the painting. "It's not that good," he says after a while.

"It is too," Samantha says. "Your dad's going to be so mad."

Aidan just shrugs and walks away. It occurs to me that being Principal Stone's son must be kind of…challenging.

Not that I feel sorry for him after how rude he was to me.

"Someone's pretty brave," Samantha says as she studies my work again.

I feel a little balloon of pride swell in my chest.

Just then Dorothy and Reza come around the corner. They walk up to look at the piece. Dorothy laughs and Reza smiles.

Samantha watches as they walk away.

"You think it's one of them?" Ashley asks. Then she pauses and says, "Who are they again?"

Oh my god.

"Dorothy Fairfield and Reza Golzar," Samantha says. "Remember? Dorothy is thinking about running for class president."

"Against Aidan? Well, that's a lost cause. Nobody even knows her."

"Ashley, she's been going to school with us since kindergarten."

Ashley knits her brows and looks at Dorothy. "Really?" She looks back at the painting. "And you think she did this?"

"Nah. She wasn't acting. She just saw it for the first time."

"And anyway," Ashley says, "a girl would never do that."

Oh my god.

Samantha surprises me again by saying, "What a dumb thing to say."

But she doesn't get into it because the bell rings.

During announcements a furious Principal Stone warns us that defacing school property could get us expelled or even arrested.

Before now I've only ever painted on abandoned ravine tunnels. When I sprayed the school wall yesterday, I felt a twinge of fear but also excitement. I'm not sure I would have done it if the brick walls hadn't already been painted. I figured it would be easy for them to paint over my piece.

But now I'm freaking out a bit. I tell myself that even if I'm arrested,

I'll probably just end up having to do community service. My mom will be mad, but she'll calm down soon enough. She's strict, but she also likes to read books with titles like *How to Talk So Kids Will Listen and Listen So Kids Will Talk*. I'll try to tap into her need to be a "cool mom" to save my skin.

I had hoped my second day here would be different than the first. Ha. On top of more barking teachers and rude students, I get slammed with a truckload of homework. In science, Mr. Green gives us five chapters to read and orders us to complete the exercises at the end of each chapter too. This is on top of finishing our class work.

I see Dorothy knit her eyebrows together. We trade glances. She told me earlier that last year the board of education decided to limit homework to an hour per night. What Mr. Green gave us will take more than an hour all by itself.

And it isn't just him. In history, we're assigned a bunch of chapters too. Reza whispers something to Dorothy, and her hand shoots up. "Ms. Adams, Mr. Green already assigned us tons of reading and questions. That and your stuff will take us two to three hours."

Ms. Adams just sighs. "Maybe you can talk to Principal Stone about that, Dorothy."

Hmm, interesting. Has Principal Stone ordered the teachers to ignore the new board policy?

"Another day, another reason to switch schools," Dorothy mutters to me as we file out of the classroom.

"Or stand up for your rights here," I say.

She and Reza look at me. Oh, crap. Have I just given away my secret identity?

Dorothy nods after a second and says, "I want to switch to a private school, but my parents want me to stay at Grayson. At least I can try to make some changes while I'm here. I was on the fence about running, but I think the students might finally be ready for change. Look at all the Tanksy buzz. I'll register as a candidate later today."

Nah. She doesn't know I'm Tanksy. And wow! I inspired her! "Awesome!" I say. "You go, girl!"

It's lunchtime, and we've arrived at our lockers. "Yo," we hear Marcus say to Aidan. "Talk to your dad. All this homework will kill us!"

Aidan shrugs. "No can do, bro."

Ox pipes up. "You'll be president soon! You've got to talk to him!"

Aidan starts yelling at Ox, and Dorothy whispers, "I can't stand Aidan, but he *is* in a weird position."

"Yeah. I've thought the same thing. I don't see how he can become school president if he doesn't protest Daddy's policies."

"Oh, don't underestimate the Aidans of the world," Reza says. He really is that rare guy who only speaks when he actually has something to say. "He's been top dog around here for a while."

"But you said he's never run for president before," I say. "What's he going to campaign about if he doesn't protest the homework?"

Dorothy says, "He'll make everything a joke. Make it seem like I'm boring and no fun for talking about real issues."

"Well, that's depressing," I say.

And that's when I realize that I'll have to keep doing my part.

Chapter Four

After lunch we have geography. At least Ms. Dear is young, new and enthusiastic. At the beginning of the class anyway. Aidan interrupts her lesson with a rant about how climate change is a hoax.

Who still thinks that?

Dorothy's calm and fact-filled response does nothing to energize the bored-looking class or stop Aidan from going on another rant. Ms. Dear tries to get him to quit talking, but she isn't nearly firm enough. This is why Aidan gets away with so much, I realize. His dad is our teachers' boss.

Then comes more homework.

After that, finally, is art.

If I thought I'd find a kindred spirit in my art teacher, I was dead wrong. Mr. George looks like he might have been a rebel at one point. He has long, shaggy hair and wears ripped jeans. But apparently life has beaten the crap out of him. Now he has a permanent sneer and a snappish tone.

"You have to learn the rules before you break the rules," is the first thing he barks at us.

Today's lesson is on perspective. Which is boring, technical stuff. But I bet a less tired teacher could find some way to make it fun.

"Not bad, Tabitha," says Samantha, sitting next to me. We're drawing a corner of the classroom after Mr. George's long, sleep-inducing lesson.

"Tanya," I say automatically. "Same," I add, referring to her sketch. Her work is technically perfect. And she's added some objects that aren't in the corner. A bullhorn and a whip.

It's a sly comment on life at Grayson.

Is there more to this girl than meets the eye?

From my other side, Dorothy says to me, "Hey, you're really good. Want to try your hand at designing a flyer for me?"

"Absolutely," I say.

I'll just have to make sure not to do it Tanksy style.

And I'll have figure out how to squeeze it in between my million hours of homework.

"What is this?" Grandpa eyes Mom's sweet-potato shepherd's pie suspiciously. It's one of my favorites. Yeah, I have a thing for sweet potatoes.

"It's shepherd's pie, Dad," Mom says.

"It's *orange*. Doesn't look like any shepherd's pie I've ever had." Grandpa takes a bite. His face looks like he's eating jailhouse slop.

"It's great, right?" I hope he'll take the hint and say something nice.

"Spicy," he grunts.

"Oh, I toned the spice right down," Mom says.

"I'm a meat-and-potatoes man, Nicole."

Mom sighs. "This *is* meat and potatoes, Dad. And a few herbs."

It takes all my willpower not to scream. I'm reminded of Mr. George's reaction to Samantha's finished drawing. He yelled at her for adding the bullhorn and whip to her picture. Like Mom, Samantha had done the thing perfectly but had also added a couple of her own touches.

What was with these dudes?

And why did my mom ever think it was a good idea for us to live with Grandpa? Yeah, I know he's having trouble on his own. I also know it will help Mom financially, and that Uncle Mike, Mom's brother, lives far away. But it seems so unfair that we have to deal with all this negativity all the time.

Grandpa tells Mom she should take a cooking course. *Oh my god*, I want to scream. *She's a fantastic cook*!

I can't stay mad at Mom. She's the one who has to spend all day with him. Once he's settled into his TV chair and we're cleaning up, I try to get her mind off him. "So," I ask, "anything interesting happen today?"

"Oh yes! Your uncle Mike called. He and Lauren are coming to town on Sunday. I'm making brunch. Don't make plans."

Clearly she thinks I've got some kind of social life. "No problem," is all I say.

I'm pretty curious to learn more about Uncle Mike. All I know is that he's a business guy. His wife, Lauren, is a teacher. Mom and I went to their wedding last year, but it was one of those huge parties, and I didn't get a chance to speak to either of them much. Mom rarely talks to or about them.

After dinner I tell her I need some air and am going to take a walk around the block.

I take a walk around several blocks.

When I get to the school, I see my *Keep Moving* piece has already been whitewashed. I do a quick painting of the Grim Reaper.

I call this one *Death by Homework*.

Chapter Five

Even at my old school I didn't have a ton of friends. That introvert thing. One day I was walking home alone. A painting on a brick wall of a woman holding out some wildflowers made me stop in my tracks. She seemed to be looking straight at me. I broke down in tears.

The next day I took a walk before dinner and came across what had to be the wildflower artist painting a new piece. She had a cardboard stencil in the shape of a tree in one hand and a can of spray paint in the other. She smiled and nodded at me. I nodded back and stayed still, watching. After a while she motioned me over and answered my dozens of questions.

After that I read everything I could about graffiti and graffiti artists. Since I was rarely invited out to movies or malls, I could spend all my allowance on cardboard and cutters and spray paint.

Soon I, too, was painting.

I'm pretty much an expert now.

This time the crowd around the piece is bigger, and way more photos are snapped. It gets a ton of attention on social media too. Samantha's post of the newest Tanksy art has two hundred likes even before the bell rings.

"It looks like a concert poster," I hear somebody say.

And Aidan Stone studies it for a while, just like last time.

Then I hear someone say, "He's really good." Why does everyone assume it's a guy? That makes me super mad.

"Wish I knew who it was," Dorothy says when we get to our lockers. "I'd get them to help on the campaign."

Ha. "Sorry you have to settle for me," I say.

"Oh god, no, I didn't mean that! You're so great! I just feel bad you don't have any help with all the art stuff!"

"I know. Just joking," I hand her the flyer sample I designed last night after I finally finished my homework. It says *Girl Boss* in big letters. In smaller letters at the bottom, it says, *Dorothy Fairfield for President.*

"Oh, wow, I love it!" Dorothy says.

"Really? I can make changes…"

"No, it's perfect! Different, but just as good as Tanksy's stuff! Would you do a brochure too? So I have something to hand out at the candidates' assembly?"

"Yeah, sure. What do you have in mind?"

Dorothy pulls her cell phone out of her backpack. "I'll send you my speech so you can grab some bullet points. I wrote it last night. My whole platform is in it."

"Sounds like a plan," I say. Then I go off to class. Between my anonymous Tanksy fame and my work for Dorothy, at least I'm making some lemonade out of a whole bunch of lemons.

Over the PA, Principal Stone, talking about my latest piece, sounds like a crazy man. I can imagine his Grinch-like eyes narrowing to laser beams.

In gym class I'm so tired that I nearly trip over my own feet during our warm-up laps.

"What's up, people?" Ms. Fife yells.

Us. All night.

In science, Mr. Green assigns four more chapters. In geography, Aidan goes on another climate-change rant. Even Dorothy is too tired to put up a fight. At least we can sleep in English. Our teacher, Mr. Freeman, is a former actor who loves the sound of his own voice. He spends the whole period reading aloud.

This is the first day food is available for sale in the cafeteria. I decide to treat myself.

"You don't seem like the fries type, Tallulah," Samantha says behind me in the line.

I turn and smile. "It's *Tanya*. I'm sure there's something besides fries."

Now she smiles. "Nope. Just chicken fingers and chicken fried steak." She leans closer and whispers, "It's not really steak. Shocker, right?"

I look at the chalkboard menu. She's right. Everything is fried. Recently a well-known local chef campaigned for better food choices in schools. Healthier and more interesting stuff. The board of education seemed all for it, but then left the choices up to the school principals. I guess Principal Stone couldn't be bothered.

"Got a problem with fries?" says Aidan. He's ahead of us in line and obviously eavesdropping.

"Nope," I say. "Love them. About once a month."

"You one of those health nuts? Girls these days. Is your friend going to campaign for kale juice in the cafeteria?"

"Oh, shut it, Aidan," Samantha says. "You might want to try some kale juice. Eating a little better might clear up your zits."

"You kidding me? Kale is gross. Anyway, nobody but chicks like you would buy it. Fries sell."

"And that's the purpose of the cafeteria?" I say. "To sell stuff to students that's bad for them?"

"Who says fries are bad for you? Show me the science! And should a cafeteria, which is basically a restaurant, be responsible for people's health?"

"Hey, genius," Samantha says, nudging him. "It's your turn."

"Rosa, you like fries, don't you?" Aidan says to the lunch lady.

"I like rice," she says.

"C'mon, Rosa, you're not in Mexico anymore!"

Oh my god.

"Fries aren't even American, Einstein. They're French," says Samantha. "*French* fries."

Okay, at least she's still calling him out.

"Nah. That's just so they sound fancy. Hey, Rosa, where are my fries?"

A glaring Rosa hurls some fries on Aidan's plate, then barks at me for my order.

Sighing, I order the chicken fingers.

Chapter Six

Sunday. Uncle Mike and Lauren's visit. Mom's done up a great brunch. Mushroom quiche, dilled potato salad, lemon-cranberry scones, fresh-squeezed orange juice and Mexican cocoa.

"What's in these eggs?" Grandpa mutters.

"Wild mushrooms," Mom says, trying to smile. "The white button ones don't have much flavor."

"And the cocoa tastes strange."

Mom sighs. "There's some cinnamon in it."

"A little too intense, Dad?" says Mike, wrinkling his nose. He reeks of cologne, so I don't think he has any business complaining. He leans toward Mom and whispers, "Maybe tone it down a bit for him?"

Wow. I'm pretty sure Grandpa can handle a few brown mushrooms and a bit of cinnamon. What are we supposed to do? Eat mashed potatoes for the rest of our lives?

Mom bites her lip, probably trying to keep herself from saying something nasty. Uncle Mike seems like another one of those people who loves to spout opinions before gathering facts. The world's full of them these days.

I see Mike and Lauren exchange a look. What the heck? How rude!

"Business good?" Grandpa asks Uncle Mike between bites of quiche. For someone who's always complaining about Mom's food, he's sure chowing down pretty hard.

"Oh yeah. Bought two more plazas."

"Fantastic."

Grandpa asks about a million more questions. Now Uncle Mike is leaning back in his chair, manspreading all over the place and talking nonstop.

At one point he turns to his wife, who's picking at the tiny amount of food on her plate, and says he couldn't do any of it without her. And how great a teacher and cook she is.

"I bet," I say. "Mom's a powerhouse too. Somehow she manages to juggle freelance work, writing her novel and taking care of the house." I don't say *and Grandpa* because I don't want to start any trouble. Unlike our guests,

I think before I speak. "And she's a great cook, too, as you can tell."

Lauren and Mike smile at me, then look at each other. They go back to talking to Grandpa.

I look at Mom. She shakes her head.

I'm out of here. I stand and say, "Well, homework calls."

I wait until Mike and Lauren have gone and Grandpa is napping before I come back downstairs. Mom is sitting at the dining table, staring at the door.

"Wow," is all I say, sitting down beside her.

She shrugs. "That's why I don't see him much."

"Why is he so…?"

"Passive-aggressive? Aggressive-aggressive? Who knows? Massive insecurity? A personality disorder?"

I figure I should change the subject. "Any more of that cocoa left?"

"Almost the whole pot," Mom says.

We pour ourselves two big mugs and then watch the first episode of a new Netflix comedy. Then we check Mom's dating profile. I make her send messages to a graphic designer, a dentist, a journalist and an engineer. So far she's only responded to messages sent to her.

"Nobody will answer," she says.

"Oh my god, they'll all answer!"

They'd better. Mom needs to get back the self-esteem Grandpa and Uncle Mike have drained out of her.

On my way over to help Dorothy make a killer campaign video, I stop by the school and do a quick sketch of Marie Antoinette eating greasy chicken fingers and fries in the guillotine and spray the words *Let them eat crap* over the latest whitewash.

Chapter Seven

I get to school early on assembly day so I have time to plaster the school hallways with flyers.

Samantha says "nice color scheme, Tandy," as I stick one on the wall by the trophy case. "Wish I'd thought of that."

I turn around. "You know, maybe you should just stop calling me by my name." I look at the flyers she's holding in her hands. "You used the same basic layout. Looks good."

"Thanks. May the best artist win." Samantha turns to go, then stops and says, "Hey, do you know about Art Makers?"

"Nope. That a band?"

Samantha rolls her eyes. "Did you come from Mars or something? It's a youth program at the art college downtown. There's a graphic art option. They offer it over the winter break and in the summer. The Design Punk guys took it a bunch of times."

This is a test. She's fishing to see if I know who the Design Punk guys are. I do, in fact, know. They're former bandmates who decided they liked designing stuff more than performing. These days they make album covers and concert posters for super-famous bands.

I point to one of her flyers and say, "Clearly, you were inspired by their design for the Four Men album cover."

She smiles. "That I was." Then she tosses her ponytail and walks away, saying, "Bye, Tanitha."

Well.

Dorothy shows up just as Samantha is leaving. "What's her deal?" she asks.

"Not sure," I murmur. "But I think she might not be as happy with her current friend group as she lets on."

Dorothy looks over her glasses at Samantha briefly, as if examining a specimen in science class. She does not seem impressed.

"The flyers look great," she says, turning back to me. "Do you have the brochures?"

"Of course." I pat my backpack hanging from my shoulder. I take a minute to survey the hall, feeling quite proud of myself.

My flyers are way better than Samantha's.

The students are pretty rowdy at the assembly, which has again been scheduled during our drama period. Everybody's probably overtired from staying up all night to finish their homework.

But I also sense that people are hyped because of the new Tanksy piece. It got double the Instalife likes as the last one did.

Principal Stone stomps to the podium and glares at us. "This is the last time I'm going to say this." He points out at the crowd with a long, thin finger. "Vandalism will get you expelled and arrested. Whoever is responsible for these disgusting acts will be caught and punished." He waits a bit before giving us a smile that looks like it hurts. "And now I'd like to introduce our presidential candidates, Mr. Aidan Stone and Ms. Dorothy Fairfield." Aidan and Dorothy make their way to the front, waving.

Here's the funny thing. I would have assumed that Aidan would be the one grinning and playing it cool. Instead, he looks uptight and scared. I think I know why. He's going to make a speech in front of everyone right after his dad, Mr. Law and Order. Dorothy, in contrast, looks relaxed and happy.

Dorothy sits on a chair beside the podium while Aidan takes his place behind it.

Aidan can't seem to decide on a facial expression. I guess he can't be too jokey because Dad is sitting two feet away. But he doesn't want to look too serious either. The result is a kind of painful-looking smile, similar to his dad's.

"Yo, people," he starts out. He gets back a big "Yo!" from the crowd. That seems to help him relax a bit. I look over at Principal Stone. *Yo* is probably a bit too "street" for him. A sign of riots to come.

Aidan points at Dorothy. "She wants to take away your fries!"

Gasps and cries of "*Noooo!*"

But Aidan is too stupid to walk away from the podium when he still has everybody in his pocket. Instead he adds, "Girls. So ridiculous. Am I right?"

This gets a lot of girls exchanging looks. Some even boo him.

Aidan just rolls his eyes. "Yeah, yeah, okay, but look at her." He points to Dorothy. "Is that who you want to represent you?"

Dorothy just tilts her head and smiles. Huge props to my girl! Others, including myself, would have lost it with Aidan publicly dissing them like that. Also, what is he even thinking? Dorothy is killing it today in a sleek white jumpsuit. I found it for her at a cool vintage boutique. Reza is Dorothy's campaign manager, but I'm responsible for all things image related. And contrary to what Aidan and Samantha think, I enjoy fashion. In point of fact, my baggy pants are way more on trend than Sam's leggings. She doesn't go downtown enough to know.

Even Aidan's friends don't seem to know how to respond. He has totally misread the student body. The kids here have been drowning in kindness and inclusion workshops since kindergarten. Even the ones who are a little monstrous themselves seem aware that Aidan has crossed a line.

He finally seems to sense it himself. Plus, he probably has nothing else to say.

I doubt he prepared a real speech. He wraps things up with a defensive "Think about it!" Then he comes out from behind the podium to some scattered laughs and applause.

He sits in the chair next to Dorothy's. Dorothy calmly gets up and walks to the podium. Once she's there, she grins, does a little shoulder shimmy and says, "Well, okay!"

The crowd bursts into applause and loud shouts of encouragement.

I glance over at a suddenly pale-looking Aidan.

Then back to my girl. Who proceeds to outline her platform in style.

She was born to do this.

She finishes up her short and sweet speech with a special surprise we've prepared.

"And about that fries thing," she says as she gives the audiovisual girl the signal to start the killer video we put together. The beginning has an interview with Tony Chase, the chef who convinced the board that the schools in the area need better food choices. He talks about the dangers of trans fats and how learning can be affected by an unhealthy diet. He then lists delicious alternatives to fried food. Curries! Stir-fries! I added some cool graphics and an upbeat soundtrack. The video ends with an adorable dance number featuring Dorothy and me and Reza, followed by a panning shot of the latest Tanksy mural. On the final black screen are the words *For real change, vote Dorothy.*

The crowd goes wild.

Dorothy flashes a peace sign and then sits back down next to a stunned Aidan. His equally pale dad walks back to the podium. It takes Principal Stone a good three minutes to get control of the room.

I catch Dorothy's eye from the audience, and we smile at each other.

We have this in the bag.

I give Mom and Grandpa a quick summary of the election assembly over dinner.

"Those artistic types just rile everybody up," grumbles Grandpa.

"That's your opinion, Dad," says Mom.

"That's a lot of people's opinions," he replies. "Including Mike and Lauren. They agree with me about a lot of things."

"Good for them," Mom snaps. "Glad I don't have to listen to their opinions. Because they're never here, are they?"

Wow, I hardly ever see Mom lose her temper. Not that she isn't justified.

She totally is. Something around here is going to have to give.

As usual, I quickly excuse myself from the table. I rejoin Mom on the couch once Grandpa is in bed.

"Hey, I never asked you about your date with the graphic designer," I say. He'd not only answered her message but also asked her out for coffee.

"Well, I learned a lot about graphic design. Way more than I needed to know."

I roll my eyes. "It's an epidemic."

"Truth," Mom says.

After dinner I head to the school to fill up that lovely white space again. I paint several coins with Dorothy's likeness on them, with the caption *Radical Change*.

Chapter Eight

The *Radical Change* piece gets triple the number of likes as my last one. And another close examination from Aidan Stone.

And on the bulletin board by the school's main doors is a flyer advertising a new school newspaper edited by Reza. He tells me it was

Tanksy who inspired him. These all seem like signs of sunnier days ahead.

Then come the announcements.

"First of all," Principal Stone says, his voice hard, "we will be installing cameras and lights around the school and locking the school gate after hours."

Ha! If I wear a ski mask, nobody will be able to tell it's me on the film. As for the lights, they don't matter. Nobody ever sees me paint because nobody hangs around our school at night anyway. It's in a weird location. Surrounded by factories. And I can easily hop a locked gate.

"Number two. There will no longer be any distribution of student-created material in the school. This is due to concerns about garbage. There will be severe penalties for any students disregarding this rule."

He sounds positively joyful when he says that. No doubt he thinks the student body will stick to the rules and turn against the revolutionaries. I seriously doubt it, given how they responded to Dorothy at the assembly. *Dude, you were there too!*

"And finally..." Stone continues.

Great. What else?

"...I have hired a vice-principal to be a visible presence in the school. Please feel free to introduce yourself to Vice-Principal Sargent as he patrols the halls."

I spot Mr. Sargent on my way to my next class. He sure lives up to his name, with military posture, an intimidating stare and a booming voice that hurts my ears.

"Your dad was pretty harsh," I hear Samantha say to Aidan at his locker at lunchtime.

Aidan just shrugs.

Samantha looks at him and frowns. "I know you don't want to defend the paper because Reza is Dorothy's campaign manager. But all students have the right to voice their opinions. Your dad is turning this school into a prison. And that might hurt your campaign. Maybe you should talk to him."

Wow! Now we're getting somewhere.

But Aidan just slams his locker shut and says, "He wouldn't listen."

Yeah, I can see that. Stone would probably ground Aidan into eternity.

I still don't feel sorry for the guy.

Well, not that sorry.

In the cafeteria, Dorothy's campaign table attracts a way bigger crowd than Aidan's. Mostly because we're giving out mini carrot cupcakes made by

Tony Chase. And—ha!—Stone and Sargent can't take them away because they're dairy-free, nut-free *and* egg-free!

Samantha did up some brochures for Aidan, but she isn't sitting at his table, which is right next to ours. Marcus and Ox are there, looking bored. Ox pulls out a coin to play table hockey with. When Aidan sees, he jabs him in the ribs and points to us.

I hear a bunch of interesting conversations while I hand out cupcakes. One between Ashley and Marcus.

"Hey, get over here, girl," Marcus says. He tries to motion Ashley away from our table.

"But they have Tony Chase cupcakes!"

"You shouldn't eat cupcakes," Marcus says. "They make you fat."

"Who cares? I'm tired of starving myself. And hey, aren't you guys pro junk food? Oh, right. Except when your girlfriends eat it, huh? Anyway, these are healthy. Lots of carrots and not a ton of sugar. Oh my god," she adds after taking a bite. "*So* good."

"No loitering," Vice-Principal Sargent barks at us. He has just stalked up to the campaign tables.

"Principal Stone gave us the okay to set up our tables here." I force myself to look him in the eye.

"Oh, he did, did he?" This guy is definitely not the kind of person to apologize. "I'll let this go today," he says, pointing at me. "But I remember the troublemakers."

Yikes.

I turn my eyes away from him and onto the next person in line for cupcakes.

I don't have to worry though. I pass Sargent a few times in the hall that after-noon, and he doesn't even glance at me.

At home I try to sort out all my homework for the evening. Five pages of science questions. Ten pages of history reading and a page of questions. Ten pages of math questions. Two pages of geography questions. And from health class, a chapter of reading and a page of questions.

Come on. Seriously?

At dinner I wasn't going to bring up our new vice-principal. I wasn't in the mood to listen to Grandpa talk about how much he likes Principal Stone's methods or the importance of order. But it turns out he's buddies with Sargent's dad.

"He's going to be a welcome addition to the school," he says.

"I don't know," I say. "It's even more depressing with him around. But on the bright side, it looks like my friend Dorothy will be elected president. She has some great ideas.

Better cafeteria food, less homework, more extracurricular activities."

"What do you want, a parade every day?" Grandpa mutters. "You're at school to learn."

I try to stay calm. "Kids learn better when they're rested and well fed. And we learn through extracurricular activities as well as classroom subjects. My friend Reza is putting together a school newspaper at home because he wasn't allowed to use a classroom or school equipment. Principal Stone won't even let him distribute it at school!"

"Really? That's awful!" Mom says.

"Well, he was probably planning to trash-talk Principal Stone," Grandpa says. "The principal was right to shut him down. And isn't Reza a girl's name?"

"No, Dad, it's not," says Mom, clearly irritated. "And who said he was going to trash-talk Principal Stone?

Anyway, there's nothing wrong with being critical. As long as you get your facts right. It encourages debate, which is healthy if done respectfully. Principal Stone sounds more like a dictator than a good leader." Mom flashes me a sympathetic look. "People are also more productive when they feel heard and valued."

"Everybody's coddled too much these days," Grandpa grumbles. "What's this?" He pokes at his food.

Mom sighs. "Chicken pot pie."

"I know that. What's the green stuff?"

"It's thyme, Dad. It won't kill you."

"I like plain food," he says.

She rolls her eyes. "No danger of anybody being coddled around here."

Later I ask Mom about her dates with the dentist and the journalist.

More sighs. "They both have kids at your school. We had different opinions about what's going on there. The Tanksy thing and all the other stuff."

Yikes. Are the adults in the community about to become as divided as their kids? I feel a little guilty. But if these guys are pro-Stone, they aren't the right guys for Mom. On the other hand, while Mom has voiced admiration for Tanksy's spirit and is clearly pro-democracy, she isn't cool with the idea of artists painting anywhere they want.

"Sorry," I say to her.

She shrugs. "Nothing to do with you."

I open my mouth and almost tell her everything, but don't.

Instead I leave the house, wearing an old puffy jacket I never wear to school.

Once at Grayson, I quickly spray the words *All fun has been canceled* in my signature Tanksy font.

My breath catches in my throat. There's a figure hovering behind a bush near the school gate.

Someone is watching me.

I gather my things and hop the fence.

I look behind me to see if I can spot who it is. I see someone step out of the bush, a tall figure with long, gray hair.

A figure that looks a lot like my art teacher, Mr. George.

Chapter Nine

I probably just imagined that whole Mr. George thing.

There's no way I can stop painting now. When it starts feeling really dangerous, I'll do what Reza did. He just took his work online.

That boy hardly ever talks, but he has a *lot* to say about Grayson. I make a mental note to ask him if he wants me to do some art for his paper.

At lunch Dorothy faces down the vice-principal in the cafeteria.

"Principal Stone's new orders," Sargent barks. "No campaign tables."

"Mr. Sargent," Dorothy says, "there is a long history of election campaigning at this school."

Ha. Dorothy told me that until this year, school elections were pretty much a joke. They're still half a joke because Aidan is Dorothy's only opponent. But at least there's one serious candidate this year.

"The print version of the school newspaper was just shut down," she continues. "This seems like a very dangerous path."

"So get a lawyer," Sargent says. "No. Tables."

"I'm surprised they didn't rip down our flyers," Dorothy mumbles as we sit at another table. She looks a little lost with nothing to do but eat lunch.

I start to tell her how Reza's online newspaper is already helping our campaign. A lot of kids I wouldn't have thought would be interested in school issues have commented on the site. But raised voices at the next table stop me.

Marcus and Ashley are fighting about something.

"Yeah, but no art and no good food," says Ashley. "It's starting to seem more like a jail than a school."

"Are you kidding me? It's just a bunch of nerds complaining!"

"In case you haven't noticed, nerds are having a moment, Marcus."

"What does that even mean?" Marcus looks very confused.

I look around the cafeteria. All around us, discussions and arguments are happening. And some people aren't sitting at their regular tables. Highly unusual.

Holy crap. We really *did* start a revolution!

This theory is confirmed when Dorothy and I go to the bathroom. Somebody has covered up the Boys and Girls signs with hand-drawn ones that say, *Whatever. Just wash your hand*s.

There's a new feeling in the halls. All of a sudden the Grayson students look completely different to me. People seem smarter, kinder, funnier. Tanksy, Dorothy and Reza did that. I feel great.

My good feeling only lasts until later that afternoon, when word spreads that Reza has been expelled. Word is, Principal Stone is threatening to sue Reza and his parents too.

I go from feeling great to feeling sick, even though I suspect Stone is bluffing. Reza was super careful not to say anything that wasn't absolutely true about anyone or that could damage their reputation.

My last class, drama, is canceled once again. I'm starting to think they're just trying to make us *think* we have a drama class. But the cancelation is a good thing today because, once again, we're overloaded with homework. I don't know how I'm going to get it all done. My stomach is churning.

Expelled. And it's all my fault.

When I get home, I go straight to my room. I tell Mom and Grandpa my stomach hurts.

I can't decide what to do. Part of me wants to come clean. It isn't fair for me to hide behind a tag. Good people like Reza are being expelled and may even be sued.

People are dying to know who Tanksy is. Well, who am I? A "good" girl or a rebel? I realize that I'm both. And one day soon I'll have to merge my two identities. But I'm not quite ready yet.

I come down for dinner. Mom announces that everything going on at my school has given her an idea for a new middle-grade novel. "It's about a girl who feels powerless in her personal life and at school. But she is secretly her school's graffiti artist!"

I stare at her. She can't know.

Can she?

No way. She'd never joke about it. She'd confront me. Not in a Mr. Sargent way, but she'd be pretty darn mad. Make me 'fess up and face the consequences.

I stare at her a bit longer. Nah, there's no way she knows. Which strikes me as funny. She hit the nail on the head with her plot summary.

It's exactly how I feel and why I do my Tanksy stuff.

Maybe Mom is feeling a little rebellious herself. No doubt she can imagine why somebody would pull a Tanksy.

She has more surprises for us. "I found a great community center not far from here. They have seniors programs. You could go a couple of mornings a week, Dad. You could meet new people, do some fun stuff. They have guest speakers and group activities. All kinds of things."

Grandpa glares at her. "Daycare."

Oh my god! I'd kill for extra-curriculars.

I escape to my room and Skype Dorothy to ask her how Reza is doing.

"Good, actually," she says. "His parents are totally in his corner. He wanted to go to the same private school

I want to go to anyway and they've agreed to send him. Maybe now my parents will finally let me go. I'm all for public education, but Grayson is the worst. Reza and I are lucky our parents can afford private school."

This makes me feel a tiny bit better.

"But maybe after you're elected, things will change."

"Maybe. But who knows? Maybe Aidan will win now. Nobody wants to risk being expelled."

"Really? You think? All our work…"

Dorothy smiles, but it's a sad smile. "It's not like we haven't seen this happen all over the world. But we have to keep fighting the good fight. Change may not come right away, but hopefully it'll come soon-ish."

I gaze at her on-screen image. Her posture is confident and her smile serene. "You'll be a great school president, Dorothy," I say.

"If I'm elected," she says. "See you tomorrow, Tanya. And thanks again for all your hard work."

"Anytime," I murmur.

Once I hear the TV, I join Mom at the kitchen table for tea.

"So?" I say. "What was the engineer like?"

"The engineer…?" she repeats after a second.

I look at her. "Yeah, the engineer."

Another pause. Then: "Oh, he was nice. But I won't be seeing him again." I can tell she doesn't want me to ask any more questions.

Mom looks a bit sad. I wonder if it's because she liked the guy but he didn't like her back.

You can't always get what you want. That's what Dorothy says. But it doesn't mean you stop trying.

I make Mom send a message to a chef. Then I kiss her on the cheek. "Got to get back to work. The race is tight. But I'm going to take a walk around the block first. Get some air."

She puts her arm around my waist and squeezes. "It's nice you're so involved with the school election."

I smile.

"Be careful," she adds. "It's getting dark out earlier."

"Of course," I say.

I paint today's slogan on the wall as quickly as I can. Just as I'm finishing up, I notice a figure in the shadows again.

If at first you don't succeed, do something illegal.

Chapter Ten

When I get to school in the morning, I see that the temporary bathroom signs have been ripped down.

I overhear Marcus commenting to Ashley, "Good. Those the people you want to hang with? The ones who want the freaks to come out of the woodwork?"

Ashley sighs. "You know, Marcus, my aunt Ivy is a university professor.

She's talked to me a lot about gender and—"

"Oh, a *professor*. Professors don't know crap."

Ashley looks at him hard. "It just doesn't seem like that big a deal to me." She turns and walks away.

These mean girls keep surprising me.

Dorothy and I spend the entire lunch break talking strategy. The debate is coming up in our last period, during our fake drama class.

Dorothy wants to promise students something new. "Something we know they'd love. Something Aidan would offer them."

"In other words, you want to compromise your ideals," I say.

"No! I'd never do that. But there must be something both camps would be in favor of."

"I think it's a bad idea. It will make us look desperate." With Reza gone, I've become Dorothy's campaign manager. "I know you don't think so, but I still think you've got this in the bag. The students may not want to risk getting expelled, but voting for you is a safe way to protest Principal Stone's policies."

"I'm not so sure about that. I think Aidan's going to focus on my 'extremism.' Make me sound like a *dangerous* choice."

"Right. Like demanding our basic rights is extreme."

Dorothy pats my arm. "Remember—"

"Yeah, I know. Change may not come right away. Blah, blah, blah."

She laughs. "That would make a great flyer. *Blah, blah, blah.*"

She's got me thinking. "You know, that's not a bad idea," I say. "*BLAH, BLAH, BLAH* in a giant font. And at the bottom, in smaller letters, *Tired of the same old, same old? Vote Dorothy for real change.*"

Dorothy laughs again. "I like it. But we can't get new flyers up before the debate, and the election's tomorrow."

"Are you kidding me? I can whip it up on my computer in half a minute flat. With some help, we can replace all the old ones before the bell rings."

"I am *so* lucky you are on my team, girl."

I grin. "Yeah, you really are."

I manage to get the new flyers done and posted as promised. They generate an instant buzz. And from the very beginning of the debate, Dorothy is masterful. Relaxed and smart-sounding but not overly nerdy. She has jokes as well as facts at her fingertips. Aidan has a couple of catchphrases. But after saying them each about six times, he starts to sound stupid, even to his own people. I see them exchanging looks and laughing.

Dorothy's summation is met with cheers.

I slump against my chair in relief. We've still got this.

"What's going on with Ashley and Marcus?" my mom asks at dinner.

"Why do you ask? And how do you even know them?"

"I sometimes bump into Ashley's mother, Jessica, at the grocery store. We struck up a conversation in line today."

"Ashley seems to like what we're all about," I say. "But Marcus is Aidan's best friend. So he automatically agrees with Aidan's ideas. Not that he actually has any."

"And that's what they've been arguing about? Her mother was so upset," Mom says. "You'd think they were thirty years old and engaged. Jessica thinks the election is going to 'tear them apart.'

Which is ridiculous. And not just because they're teenagers. If their values are so different, they're probably not suited for each other."

"Or one of them is crazy," Grandpa says. "In this case, this Ashley girl. Trying to tell everybody what's good for them."

"Dad!" Mom says.

"I'm on Ashley's side too, Grandpa," I say. "Do you think *I'm* crazy?"

"Tanya," Mom warns.

"Everybody's crazy around here!" Grandpa suddenly yells. He points to my mom. "And her! She's just like that Ashley girl! Trying to tell me what's good for me! Putting me in daycare! It's elder abuse!"

"Oh my god," I explode, standing up and pointing. I'm so mad, I can barely get the words out. "*You're* the one abusing *her*!"

"Tanya!" Mom cries.

But I run to my room and slam the door.

I sneak out later to get my painting done. Still furious, I scrawl *I fought the law and I'd better win* on my big white canvas. A nod to Banksy and a reference to an old song Reza told me about. Not only does he listen to people, he also listens to a whole lot of music.

I don't even care if anyone is watching me.

Chapter Eleven

Election day. Lunchtime. Voting time. After lunch, Vice-Principal Sargent will count the ballots. The outcome will be announced in second-last period.

"Oh, great. Voter intimidation," Dorothy says. She points in the direction of the voting booth. A bunch of Aidan's friends are standing beside it, being super obnoxious. They're asking people who they're going to vote for and dissing them if they say Dorothy. I see a couple of quiet types change direction when they realize what's happening.

Dorothy starts to get up from our table, but I put a hand on her arm. "Better for you to stay here. I'll go." I walk toward the booth. "Hey, guys. You know you can't do this. It's called voter intimidation."

"What are you talking about?" Marcus says. "We're just being our normal, happy selves."

The vice-principal is standing right there.

"Mr. Sargent…"

"You heard him," Sargent says. "Nothing wrong with a little enthusiasm."

Wow. Just…wow.

The afternoon is torture.

But in history, Ms. Adams surprises the class with a brief history of voter suppression in our region.

And Mr. Freeman's read-aloud choice is a collection of Langston Hughes poems, including one about holding fast to dreams.

All this gives me a little more hope for humanity, which had pretty much disappeared when I started attending Grayson.

Finally the election result is announced. Aidan has won by *two* votes. School bylaws insist on a recount if there is less than a ten-vote spread. The recount will be overseen by past president Lucas Jones.

"Great," Dorothy says, dropping the brave smile she had plastered on. "Lucas and Aidan are neighbors, and their parents play golf together. Plus, he's a troublemaker. If he was anybody else, he'd have been expelled by now."

"Whoa," I say. "So can we protest him being in charge of the recount?

That's a conflict of interest, right? So shady!"

"We can try. But in case you haven't noticed, this school's whole administration is shady."

As soon as the end-of-class bell rings, we run to the office.

Only to get yelled at by the vice-principal. "Why aren't you girls on your way to class?"

"We're concerned about the recount being done by Lucas Jones." Dorothy looks Sargent right in the eye. *So brave!* "We feel that's a conflict of interest. Lucas and Aidan are friends."

"Are you questioning their ethics? Or the ethics of this administration?" Sargent's eyes narrow.

"Not at all," Dorothy lies. "Just the opposite. I know this administration wants to do everything it can to ensure a fair election result."

Not just brave. Smart.

Just then Principal Stone comes out of his office. "Trouble here, Mr. Sargent?"

Sargent crosses his arms. "These young women are saying that Lucas Jones should not be in charge of the recount."

"Oh, is that so? Show a little respect, girls. We know what we're doing. Now run along to class."

So much for democracy.

After the recount, we learn that Aidan has actually only won by a single vote. Dorothy says there's no point asking for another recount.

"But what if Aidan starts doing crazy stuff once he's in power?"

"He might. Although his whole platform was based on french fries, so I doubt it. But if he starts doing terrible things, we'll make our voices heard."

I look at her. "You're my hero, you know that?"

"Right back at you, Tanya," she says.

Wow. And she doesn't even know about my secret rebel work.

Or does she? Just before we part ways, Dorothy winks at me.

"It's horrible. The Stones just do whatever they want," I say at dinner after telling Mom and Grandpa all the election drama of the day.

"Give people power and that's what happens," Grandpa says. Which confuses me a little because it's pretty much the opposite to everything he's been saying about the election so far. But then he points at Mom. "I invite my daughter to come live with me, and she becomes a dictator!"

Ah.

"Dad!" Mom says sharply. "That's an awful thing to say! I'm trying to take care of you!"

"Yeah, Grandpa," I say.

"I went to that daycare place this morning and I'm not going again," he says, banging his fist on the table. "You can't make me."

"No," Mom says, sighing. "I can't make you. But you know, I watched you. And you didn't seem to mind it when you were there. You've just been stewing since you got home. Honestly, I think it's the fact that I'm right about something that's bugging you."

"That's crazy," Grandpa huffs. "I didn't like it at all. I was treated like an old man. I had to talk to a social worker!"

"Jason is amazing!" Mom says. "He's so passionate about his work. He just wanted to figure out what kind of things you like to do."

I look at her. She already seems very chummy with *Jason*.

Hmm…I'll definitely be keeping an eye on that situation. I need a distraction to keep me from thinking about the lost election.

But in the meantime…

I head out to the school. No sign of my stalker tonight. I paint likenesses of the *Stranger Things* cast with the caption *Life in the Upside Down*.

Chapter Twelve

There's an assembly first thing Monday morning.

I'm not the only one who cries at Dorothy's concession speech.

Even Aidan's supporters are quiet when he steps up to the mic and speaks. Maybe because all he says is, "If a thing ain't broke, don't fix it, am I right? *Fries!*" Then he walks off the stage, arms raised in victory, to faint applause.

It seems his followers are finally realizing that even a junior-high-school government should be more than a joke.

Dorothy may not have been able to do much as school president, but Aidan's people might be recognizing that she would have given it a great shot. For sure she would have submitted an official complaint to the board of education about how Principal Stone isn't following the homework policy. Or the healthy-eating guidelines proposed by chef Tony Chase. She's still planning to do it, but her complaints will have less impact without the presidential title.

Maybe it's finally sinking in for everyone that now Aidan is going to be representing our school at regional student council meetings...

I feel a tap on my shoulder as we quietly file out of the gym.

I turn around to see Samantha. "You did a good job, Tatiana."

"Tanya," I say automatically.

"Hey, did you ever apply to Art Makers?"

I had completely forgotten about that.

"No. Thanks for reminding me."

"You're too late for the winter-break session, but they just opened applications for summer. Get on it, girl. Spots go super fast. I'm doing the first two weeks in July."

Wow, she's actually being friendly.

"Well, okay then."

"Off to geography. Later."

With that, she flashes me the *Hunger Games* salute.

Double wow.

A thought suddenly strikes me. Was Samantha trying to sabotage Aidan with her not-so-great flyers and brochures? Her art-class work is a billion times better than the stuff she did for him.

Did she even vote for Aidan? My gut and that *Hunger Games* salute say no.

Speaking of *The Hunger Games*…boy, does Grayson ever feel like the Capitol now.

I suspect Principal Stone has ordered our teachers to assign us even more homework.

They seem as tired as we do.

Today Mr. Green practically sets a fire demonstrating a chemistry experiment.

Ms. Fife trips twice while doing warm-up laps with us in gym.

Our math teacher, Mr. Gibbs, keeps muttering, "Excuse me, that's wrong" after mixing up mathematical formulas.

Mr. Freeman practically puts *himself* to sleep while reading aloud.

In geography class, Ms. Dear's voice breaks as she talks about rain clouds.

In history, Ms. Adams keeps trailing off and staring out the classroom window. Maybe she's picturing an imaginary school where principals actually follow board policy.

And in art class, Mr. George yells a whole lot less than usual.

But everybody's energy level skyrockets when the bell rings at the end of the day. We clear that place out in about twelve seconds.

Grandpa tries a different tactic tonight. Angry silence and zero eye contact. He doesn't even answer when I ask how his second morning at the community center went.

Mom and I roll our eyes at each other.

At least his silent treatment means he can't complain about Mom's cooking. She's gone a little heavy on the hot sauce, even for me. It's breakfast for dinner night. Kicked-up scrambled eggs. Spicy but still delicious.

"How was the current-events group?" I ask Grandpa. I'm going to force him to talk to me whether he wants to or not. "What was today's topic?" I wait a couple of seconds before prompting him again. "Grandpa?"

"Middle East," he finally mumbles. He still isn't making eye contact.

"Oh boy, that must have been barrels of fun. Were the other people nice at least?"

"No," he grunts.

Mom and I look at each other again. She shrugs.

Once he's in his TV chair and Mom and I are in the kitchen cleaning up, I say, "Well, we wanted him to shut up."

"Tanya!" Mom says. But she smiles slightly.

I wonder if she'll be able to get him to go to the center again. I don't see how, but I hope so. For his sake but also so Mom has a reason to see that Jason guy again. I have a good feeling about him.

Things are bleak, but I have to believe they'll get better someday, like Dorothy always says they will.

Tonight's tagline, under a painting of a book, is *Just Another Chapter*.

Chapter Thirteen

Ox plops down beside me during lunch.

"What's that?" He makes a face at my food.

"Falafel and pita."

"Jew food." He practically spits the words.

More sharp pains in my chest. I had a feeling this would happen.

The election of Aidan has given his friends permission to say whatever they think.

It's super depressing to think these impulses bubble under people's skins, and that it's just good leaders who keep them in check.

But I don't have a sharp reply ready. "Everybody likes falafels, Ox," is all I can think to say.

Dorothy jumps in. "Why don't you go sit with your friends if our food is bothering you so much?" She holds up her wrap. "Curried chickpea roti. Want some? Delicious. My uncle Jay's recipe."

"Gross. Think I will. Sit with the normal people, I mean." Ox looks at our wraps in disgust.

Wow. I guess he came over here with the sole purpose of harassing us.

Today we're sitting close to the lunch counter. Rosa's been watching us. As soon as Ox gets up, she nods to her two staff, who go outside through the door by the cash register. They come back a couple of minutes later carrying huge trays of...burritos?

After that come trays of jerk chicken, coleslaw and rice with beans!

Was this all made by the cafeteria ladies?

There are oohs and ahs from the kids in line.

Ashley is first up.

"Yay, are those homemade burritos? I love those!"

"No you don't," Marcus growls behind her.

"How would you know?" Ashley sticks out her chin. "We only ever eat what *you* want to when we're not in school. And when we're here, there's usually no choice." Turning to Rosa, Ashley says, "I'll have the burritos, please."

Marcus turns red. "This is stupid."

"Yes, it is," Ashley retorts. "It's stupid that this cafeteria has only ever offered chicken fingers and fries! And a couple of other things that look a lot like chicken fingers and fries! It's also stupid that Aidan and his dad are totally against any other options."

Marcus looks shocked for a second, then says, "You know what's really stupid? Us! I'm done!"

"Oh no you don't," she yells as he walks away from her. "I was done with you first!"

Just then Principal Stone storms into the cafeteria. Aidan must have slipped out to tell his dad about Rosa's little stunt since Vice-Principal Sargent, who usually patrols the cafeteria at lunch, is away today.

I look at Rosa, worried about what will happen next.

She winks at me just as a woman carrying a microphone and a guy with a video camera walk in through the side door. I recognize her. She's a reporter from the local morning talk show.

The reporter sticks a microphone in Principal Stone's face. "Hello, Principal Stone, and may I say bravo? I'm Jen Wong from *Morning in the City*. Can you tell our viewers what inspired you to provide more nutritious and culturally diverse school food in your cafeteria?"

I can't hear what Stone mumbles. Something about how his students deserve the best and he's trying to make a point with the board of education. Blah, blah, blah.

And then the reporter sticks her microphone in Aidan's face. He looks stunned. Beside him, Ox starts to yell about his right to eat "normal" food. But Aidan jabs him in the ribs. Ox looks confused but shuts up immediately. Then a pink-faced Aidan says something about how he was recently elected school president and how the opposition convinced him that better cafeteria food is a good idea. It's a flat-out lie, but the Aidan types of the world will do anything to save their skins. At least this one will have a good outcome.

I stare at Rosa and the rest of the grinning lunch ladies.

More heroes.

And then another miracle happens.

After lunch, once we've all settled down in art class, Mr. George looks around the room and then says, "Okay, we need to take a break from the technical work. It's time for some soul stuff. Your next assignment is to draw or paint a flower. In whichever medium you prefer. Use whatever we have in the room. There isn't much. But limitation sometimes leads to innovation. Draw any flower. A rose, a daisy, a weed. In any state. Living, dying, dead. Make it an expression of you. Your innermost thoughts. Your feelings. Right now."

The room is silent. But Mr. George doesn't seem to notice. He just continues on. "I know it can be scary to put yourself out there. To put your feelings on display. But that's how artists connect with and influence people. And how they drive change."

Holy crap. Maybe it *was* him who was watching me do my rebel graffiti all those nights.

The messages are getting through.

The adults are finally being adults.

The room suddenly starts humming with excitement.

Mr. George grins. "Well, what are you waiting for?" He motions toward the supply shelf. "Get going!"

After art, there is yet another miracle. Ms. Adams gives us barely any homework in history!

I practically skip home.

From the minute I walk in, it's obvious that Mom and Grandpa have been snapping at each other all day.

I bubble over with my news. The day started out so bad but ended with such glorious signs of resistance!

"Those lunch ladies should be fired," Grandpa mutters.

"Oh, I'm sure they will be," Mom says. "Heaven forbid people try new things."

"Why should they be forced to?" Grandpa snaps back.

"Who's forcing anybody?" Mom yells.

"You are!"

"We're not talking about you! But since you want to, who's forcing *you* to do anything? We didn't even go out today!"

I gulp down my dinner in seconds and escape to my room, as usual.

I do about a million flower sketches before going out for my nightly paint. Tonight I paint a few flowers around the words *Flower Power* on the school wall.

I pack up my gear. I turn around and nearly scream as I find myself face-to-face with my stalker.

It isn't Mr. George.

It's Aidan Stone. The hood on his jacket has shaggy fake-fur trim. In the shadow of the bush, it looked like my watcher had long, shaggy hair. Aidan is tall for his age. Mr. George is short for his. They're the same height.

Crap.

"You're really good," he says.

"Thanks. I take it you're going to tell everyone. Why haven't you before now?"

"I didn't want to bust you," he says. "I like your stuff." He pauses. "You know, I paint a bit too. Secretly. At home."

I have no doubt he has to hide his hobby from his dad, who thinks art is for sissies.

"I actually admire you," Aidan continues. "You took a risk. Yeah, I did think about outing you when it was looking like Dorothy was going to win the election. Then I won. But today…"

Don't bust me, don't bust me, don't bust me…

"You humiliated me."

"What? I didn't call that reporter!" I say. "Rosa probably did. But you should be on your knees thanking her. She made you look like a hero."

Aidan shakes his head. "I had to say Dorothy made me change my mind. I didn't want to look like an idiot."

"You didn't. And that's not humiliation! You humiliate people in much worse ways."

"Well, I felt humiliated. And I don't humiliate people. I kid around."

"Your 'jokes' aren't funny."

"You activists. No sense of humor."

I don't bother pointing out that Ox certainly hadn't been kidding around. I'd never win an argument with this guy. He'd never listen to anybody but himself.

"So when are you going to tell your dad?"

"Probably tonight."

I take a breath and nod. "Okay."

"He'll probably expel you tomorrow. But I'll try to talk him out of pressing criminal charges."

I take another breath and nod again. "Okay."

And with that, I head home.

I sense Aidan's eyes on me for a long time.

But I don't turn back.

Chapter Fourteen

I don't tell Mom or Grandpa that I'm about to become infamous. A tiny part of me hopes I won't get expelled. That Aidan will decide to do the right thing. Which is to keep his big mouth shut.

But, of course, my hopes are dashed. Principal Stone calls me to his office not two minutes after the morning bell.

He's calm. The calmest I've ever seen him. "I think you know why you're here, Miss Kofsky. You're the vandal. And therefore I will be expelling you. You're lucky that I'm not pressing charges. I've called your mother. She's on her way."

I feel sick to my stomach.

Mom is quiet when she arrives. But I can tell she's furious. She also looks and sounds as if she's trying to hold back tears.

I feel even sicker.

She only looks at me to ask, "Is it true?"

"Yeah," I whisper.

She signs some papers Stone shoves at her. Then the principal hands me a garbage bag and tells me to clean out my locker and return my textbooks to the office.

As soon as we're out in the hall, Mom says, "I'll wait in the car while you empty your locker."

I can't say anything. I just nod.

One silver lining: everybody's in class.

Once I get to the car, Mom finally lets loose. She screams and screams and screams. She trusted me. What was I thinking, risking getting arrested? And what about walking to school alone at night? That area is deserted after hours. Something really bad could have happened…

I don't say anything. I just let her get it all out.

When we get home, she shuts off the car and sighs. "I understand where the impulse came from, but you made some really bad choices, Tanya."

I nod. She isn't wrong.

Of course, Grandpa asks why I'm home from school so early. Mom tells him.

Now it's his turn to rant and rave. Not just about me but also about what a terrible parent my mom is.

That's it. Mom finally gives it right back to him. "*How dare you?*" she says quietly. "I'm a far better parent than you or Mom ever were. Both of you were so critical of everything I did. I had absolutely no confidence or self-esteem. And whenever I pushed back, I was told I was too sensitive! Maybe you were too mean. Ever think of that?"

"Yeah, you're mean, Grandpa," I add. "Sometimes I leave the house just to get away from you!"

Mom whirls around. "You don't get to talk right now." She's right. I should just keep quiet.

Grandpa is holding the gigantic cell phone Mom gave him. "Well, let's hear what Mike has to say about all this!" He punches some numbers.

"Oh yes, let's," Mom says. "I *really* value his opinion."

Oh wow, this is not going to go well. How did this Tanksy thing explode into a huge family blowout? I continue to keep my mouth shut.

Soon Uncle Mike is on speaker-phone, yelling at both me and Mom. Something about her bad choices making me this way.

Excuse me? What bad choices? And what way?

Suddenly Mom sighs and goes very quiet. "I can't do this anymore," she says.

"Do what?" Grandpa barks.

"Live with you. Or even talk to you. Either of you." I know she means my uncle, not me. "I need a break."

"Yeah, right," says Mike over the speaker. "Where will you go?"

"This may come as a huge shock, Mike, but I am actually capable of supporting myself and my daughter. My freelance work may not be high-paying, but we don't live big." Mom turns to me. "Go pack a few things. We're getting a hotel for the night."

"Oh, that's a great idea," says Grandpa. "Reward her bad behavior."

"And then we can have a good long talk," Mom says to me, completely ignoring Grandpa.

"What about Dad?" Mike asks. Smart guy. He sounds a little panicked now. He knows what's coming.

"Well, Mike," says Mom calmly, "I guess you're going to have to make your way here. I'm sure you'll come up with a terrific plan for the future. You have lots of ideas, right? Ideas that are so much better than mine. And you two get along so well." Man, my mom can really dish it.

I run upstairs to pack.

Before we leave I paint *Tanksy out* in a corner of my closet.

Chapter Fifteen

Before long Mom and I find a cute and affordable apartment a little farther downtown. Mom insists I take the bedroom. Teens need their space, she says. She tells me she's lived in small places all her life and doesn't mind sleeping on the pullout couch. The apartment is super close to an arts-based public school. I make friends practically the minute I step inside. These are my people, I think.

There were a few days between getting kicked out of Grayson and my first day at the new school. I thought I might be able to catch up on all the sleep I'd missed from too much homework, helping Dorothy and sneaking out to spray-paint. But Mom wasn't having any of that. My "consequence" was that I had to paint the whole apartment.

I actually felt a pretty huge sense of accomplishment when it was done. And then Mom let me create a mural on one of my bedroom walls. I painted a dandelion sprouting from a crack in the sidewalk. It was the flower painting I never got to finish for Mr. George. When Mom saw it, her eyes watered and she gave me a big hug. "You're amazing, you know that?"

It's been a pretty insane few weeks, but things are settling down. Mom has started dating that social worker, Jason. Which is fine. I liked him as soon as I met him.

Through him we find out that Mike and Lauren have installed a full-time caregiver for Grandpa at his house. And, will you look at that, the caregiver is taking him to the community center twice a week. Apparently, he's happy to go now because he's met a "lady friend" there!

The miracles keep happening. About a month after we move out, Grandpa phones and apologizes to both of us. Mom invites him and his lady friend, whose name is Sally, to dinner one night. We send a cab to pick them up. And the night is really fun. Sally is a nonstop chatterbug. Maybe that's the secret to happiness with Grandpa. Not letting him talk. He doesn't seem to mind. In fact, he seems like a whole new person. Those old guys need their mates.

Dorothy and I keep in touch. She ended up switching to Reza's school for second term, where it looks like she's meeting a whole bunch of her future cabinet members. Her Instalife feed is filled with photos of youth leadership summits and such.

When I'm not hanging out with my arty new friends, I'm enjoying our cool new neighborhood. One day I bump into Samantha. She's wearing pants even baggier than mine and a T-shirt with a hairless cat on it and the caption *All Cats Are Beautiful*.

"I like your shirt," I say.

She grins. "Thanks. My own design. There are loads of others. I just sold a ton of them to school friends. I was inspired by you, Tanksy! I can do what I love to make a statement *and* a little money." She tapped the side of her forehead. The universal signal for smart.

She is. Obviously political T-shirts are banned at school. The message on hers is subtle, but it represents respect for diversity.

"Well. Who would have thought Samantha Pimm would end up carrying the activist banner at Grayson?"

"Activist? I'm an entrepreneur, baby. My Instalife is *on fire*."

I smile. "Right." Good for her. She's doing her. Getting the message out in her own way. "Good luck," I tell her. "Nice seeing you."

"Nice seeing you too. Oh, hey, did you ever apply to Art Makers?"

"Yeah, I did. But I can't do the same two weeks as you. My mom and I are renting a cabin up north for a couple of weeks at the beginning of July."

"Oh, too bad. Aidan's doing it too, you know."

I blink. "What?"

Samantha grins. "You know he paints, right? He told his dad he wants to be an artist. The Grinch had a fit, as you can imagine. But apparently now he's okay with it. Aidan even managed to talk him into getting better art supplies at Grayson. Said he couldn't make it big if he wasn't properly prepared." She winks. "He might call you. You inspired him too. And he feels bad about…the other stuff. He's talked to his people. He even made a speech at the winter assembly about how insulting people is wrong and that everyone should be treated the way they'd like to be treated."

"Oh…wow!"

She smiles. "Later, Tanya." She gives me a quick hug and walks away. I stare at her back for a while, then turn in the opposite direction, toward home.

Once there, I think about how far I've come since I first met Samantha.

How far we've both come. And in a corner of my new closet I paint a tiny caption, in the perfect calming shade of ocean blue.

Keep the Faith.

Acknowledgments

Okay, my pet peeve is the acknowledgments page that lists a thousand people. (Ooooh, you're sooooo popular!) So I'm just going to thank the whole spectacular team at Orca, as well as the entire awesome Toronto kid lit community. I'm ugly crying just thinking about all you gorgeous souls.

 Bev Katz Rosenbaum is the author of several works of fiction. She has worked in-house as an editor for book publishers and magazines and has taught writing at the college level. Currently she juggles writing children's books with freelance editing. Bev lives in Toronto.